Cynthia Hernandez

My Friend Kat

To order additional copies of this book, contact:
Xlibris
844-714-8691
www.Xlibris.com
Orders@Xlibris.com

ISBN: Softcover   978-1-6698-7940-4
         EBook   978-1-6698-7939-8

Print information available on the last page

Rev. date: 06/26/2023

My Friend Kat

My name is Macy & my best friend is Kat, we go to school together, but she is not in the same class as me, Kat and I met at recess and she was sitting alone with her teacher's aide.

Kat is not like the other kids, but she is nice and loves to draw like me. Kat is also very smart. She is the best student in the class. She even knows how to do math at a high level, and she is a Genius. She even helps me with my math.

However, sometimes Kat gets sad and I do not like it when she gets sad. The other kids made fun of Kat because she has Down syndrome. One afternoon, Kat and I were playing hopscotch and the popular girls came over, we asked them if they want to play but they said no, they wanted to invite us to sleep over, kat and I were so excited. We only have sleepovers with each other, so it was nice making more new friends.

The next day was Friday, Kat came over to my house so we can get some things for our sleepover, we bought new sleeping bags and PJ's, and we even baked some cupcakes to bring for everyone.

The day of the sleepover has finally arrived and we could not be more excited. Ashely, the most popular girl in school welcomed us inside her house. It was big and her room was perfect like a princess castle. They had all types of snacks and food for us to eat; they even had board games for us to play.

Kat and I were having so much fun with our new friends then it was time to watch a movie, "Toy Story", it was Kat and I favorite movie, we got even more excited, it couldn't get better than this. In the middle of the movie. Kat went to use the restroom and Ashley turned to me along with the other girls and told me they only wanted me at the party, not Kat but her mom said she had to invite her because she was different and does not have many friends.

Just hearing what Ashley said me made me so angry but we were stuck there until morning.

Ashley said if I want to be popular like them. I can't be friends with Kat anymore. I was so sad! How could they be so mean, Kat is the best! She is a great friend I could never leave her, I looked at Ashley and told her, I'll think about it, but little does she know I was not going to betray my friend for them. I would rather have one nice friend than 10 new mean friends. Kat came back from the restroom and sat next to me, she told me she is having the best time, and that she was so happy to be my friend. I hugged Kat and told her BFF, best friends forever.

13

The very next day, we all got up just in time for our parents to pick us up & we all went home. It was not until Monday at the playground that we bumped into Ashley and her friends again.

15

Ashley came right up to me with a smile on her face & pulled me next to her, and then pushed Kat on the ground and told her that I did not want to be her friend anymore.

I was so angry & Kat started crying. I turned around and told Ashley to stop, I only have one friend, and she is the best; her name is Kat, Ashley was so angry she did not like that. I told Ashley you need to be nicer to people and not be mean and treat others the way you want to be treated. I grabbed Kat's hand and gave her a hug. I told her, I would never leave my best friend.

Ashley said to me I will never be one of them then one of the girls from the group said she wanted to be friends with me & Kat and she did not like how Ashley push Kat on the ground because she has a sister like Kat and wouldn't like to see someone do that to her.

As soon as one by one, each girl said they wanted to be our friend.

Ashley was standing there all alone & Kat looked at her, walked right up to her and pulled out her hand & said, you do not have to be mean. We can all be friends, just be nice to everyone & you can be happy too. Ashley sees how everyone was on our side & Kat forgave her and offered to be her friend even after being so mean.

Ashley felt awful and cried, "I am so sorry & I will never be mean again. Kat hugged her and said, remember to treat others the way you want to be treated.

THE END.

Printed in the United States
by Baker & Taylor Publisher Services